SEEKERS

Hope and Disappointment on the Border

Patricia Sutton

ReferencePoint Press

San Diego, CA

For more information, contact:
ReferencePoint Press, Inc.
PO Box 27779
San Diego, CA 92198
www.ReferencePointPress.com

LIBRARY OF CONGRESS CATALOGING-IN-PUBLICATION DATA

Names: Sutton, Patricia, author.
Title: Asylum seekers : hope and disappointment on the border / by Patricia
    Sutton.
Description: San Diego, CA : ReferencePoint Press, Inc., 2023. | Includes
    bibliographical references and index.
Identifiers: LCCN 2022002232 (print) | LCCN 2022002233 (ebook) | ISBN
    9781678203245 (library binding) | ISBN 9781678203252 (ebook)
Subjects: LCSH: Refugees--United States--Juvenile literature. | Asylum,
    Right of--United States--Juvenile literature.
Classification: LCC JV6601 .S88 2023 (print) | LCC JV6601 (ebook) | DDC
    323.6/31--dc23/eng/20220318
LC record available at https://lccn.loc.gov/2022002232
LC ebook record available at https://lccn.loc.gov/2022002233

CONTENTS

INTRODUCTION

From above, the area near the Del Rio–Ciudad Acuña International Bridge looked like some sort of festival. Portable toilets stretched out in long rows, and colorful tents sprang up in the dry Texas dirt. Men cut sturdy carrizo cane from the riverbanks to build lean-to and hut frames, and they draped brightly patterned blankets over them to shelter the surging crowds. The sounds of children playing, babies crying, and people milling about filled the dusty air. So did the smell of garbage, piles of which had been left to rot in the triple-digit temperatures. This, however, was no festival; all of the people huddled under the bridge were trying to enter the United States in search of a better life. Most had come from the island nation of Haiti—the poorest country in the Western Hemisphere. Many others, who had resided in southern Mexico, came too. Hundreds of people arrived at the encampment each day, eventually growing the group's numbers to over fifteen thousand.

One Family's Story

Gibbens and Lugrid Revolus, along with their two-year-old son, Diego, were among the crowd at this US border with Mexico, hoping to be granted asylum. Asylum is protection offered by a government to people who fear that remaining or returning to their home country will cause them serious harm. In 2018, the couple left Haiti for Chile, in South America, hoping to find work to support themselves. For a while, things improved for them, but eventually the Chilean economy worsened, and people there started to resent outsiders like the Revolus family for taking their jobs. Gibbens explains that attitudes had changed toward Haitians: "We faced discrimination and racial slurs." When two coworkers tried to stab him—and his boss refused to intervene—Gibbens and Lugrid decided it was time to move again. "It wasn't an easy decision," Gibbens says, "but we were desperate."[1]

The family traveled for nearly three months. They scraped together enough money to ride buses most of the way, but they were forced to walk many days with their toddler. They boarded a jam-packed boat to cross from Co-

lombia to Panama, and then they made their way north through Central America and into Mexico. When they arrived in Del Rio, Texas, they carried hope that their lives would change. After all, rumors had spread that newly elected US president Joe Biden would ease restrictions at the border.

People were given numbered tickets in order to be processed by American immigration officials. There were different colors for four categories: single men, single women, pregnant women, and families with young children. Then they all waited. As the thousands of migrants struggled to find food and water on the US side of the border, streams of people waded back through the murky waters of the Rio Grande to the Mexican side. There, they purchased what they could afford and trudged back to the encampment. Hoisting cases of water or soda over their heads, carrying crying babies, and bags filled with food and diapers, they returned to their tents and waited.

A Dream Denied

The situation had reached a crisis point, but the Revolus family did not know that. The United States did not have the manpower to process all those gathered, nor did they intend to let everyone in. Things had gotten out of hand. Images of US Border Patrol agents on horseback, grabbing a migrant by the shirt, using the ends of the horse reins like a whip to keep people from crossing the river, went viral. It is unclear how decisions were made, or exactly how many migrants were released into the United States.

Haitian migrants rest near the Del Rio–Ciudad Acuña International Bridge in Del Rio, Texas, on September 17, 2021. Many migrants waited in an encampment there for months, hoping to be granted asylum.

Some of the most vulnerable were allowed in, including unaccompanied children, pregnant women, and single mothers with young children. But many others were denied entry.

On September 24, 2021, authorities moved in and cleared the makeshift camp. That day, Border Patrol officers moved the Revolus family to a detention center, where they spent a few days in confinement before receiving a decision: the family was denied entry to the United States. Soon thereafter, they boarded a bus to the airport and were deported, or returned, to Haiti. "We were not given the chance to make our case for asylum," says Gibbens. "We were just looking for a better life, but we were turned back."[2] Although the exact numbers are unknown, Secretary Alejandro

Mayorkas of the US Department of Homeland Security reported that approximately two thousand detainees had been deported to Haiti. Another eight thousand migrants had voluntarily returned to Mexico. The government allowed the rest to remain in the United States.

Each journey to asylum is unique. Some travelers meet with success, but others suffer the same fate as Gibbens Revolus. Many wait for years in the United States or Mexico for their cases to be heard, and all the while their lives are on hold. The *National Law Review* reports that the immigration court system faces a backlog of more than 1.3 million asylum cases, but that does not stop those who are desperate from coming. The situations they face at home leave them no choice. They come filled with hope for a better life, but many find deep disappointment instead.

CHAPTER ONE

The Root Causes for Seeking Asylum

People have always migrated. Some are pulled to a new place by a new job, a better economy, a change in climate, or to be near family. Others are pushed out by war, gang violence, political corruption, natural disasters, or domestic abuse. They flee to survive.

Some of these survivors receive refugee status while still living in their own countries. The United Nations Convention Relating to the Status of Refugees and its 1967 Protocol define a refugee as a person who is unable or unwilling to return to his or her home country due to past persecution or fear of being persecuted "on account of race, religion, nationality, membership in a particular social group, or political opinion."[3] War, hunger, and climate change have created social catastrophes that have grown the refugee population.

Like refugees, people who seek asylum also believe their lives are in danger, but they have not received official refugee status that protects them. They flee because they have suffered persecution at home. Asylum seekers from Central and South America, the Caribbean, and Mexico arrive at the US border to plead their cases to be granted asylum and protection from being deported to their homeland.

Not everyone who seeks asylum qualifies for it. Some arrive at the southern border lacking official identification and necessary paperwork to show proof of persecution. Not all of them understand the requirements. The process can be complicated, inconsistent, and confusing. What these people do know, however, is that their lives, and those of their family, are in danger.

Each asylum seeker's story is unique. Whether suffering persecution because of political beliefs, gang or gender-based violence, or desperate conditions due to economic or natural disasters, the reason for seeking asylum begins at home.

Bárbara: Political Persecution

The First Amendment to the US Constitution protects freedom of speech and the right to peacefully protest. Not all countries offer that same protection to their citizens, however, which is one reason people seek asylum in the United States.

Participating in a political protest is what sent a Nicaraguan woman named Bárbara on her path toward asylum. In 2018, Bárbara and her brother joined hundreds of thousands of protesters in a Mother's Day march in Managua, Nicaragua. She knew it might be dangerous, but she never imagined the impact it would have on her life. Wearing the blue and white of her country's flag, she and the other demonstrators filled the main street. Led by a group of women, the mile-long crowd marched to honor sons and daughters who had been gunned down by President Daniel Ortega's government. The president's increasing power as an authoritarian ruler threatened workers, the environment, and the elderly, and on September 29, 2018, he had declared political protests illegal. Still, Bárbara, a young single mother and store owner, decided she needed to lend her support to the movement. "That was the beginning of the end. From that, my entire life changed,"[4] said Bárbara.

Along the way, gunfire disrupted the march, sending protesters fleeing in all directions. Bárbara lost track of her brother and retreated to her store, locking the door behind her. A group of young people running down the street caused a commotion. Sensing they were probably students from the nearby university, she opened the door and urged them to come in. Bárbara hoped that no one noticed that she let in twenty-one protesters. They squeezed inside waiting for several hours, until it was safe for them all to leave.

Two days later she returned alone to her shop. Almost immediately, two Toyota Hilux trucks screeched to a stop in front of the store. These pickup trucks, known to the people as "death trucks," belonged to the paramilitary and contained pro-government supporters who roamed the streets looking for people who dared to protest against Ortega. Someone called out Bárbara's name, and she froze. When she turned around, she was surrounded by the drivers. It was clear that someone had seen her give shelter to the protesters on the day of the march. One of the thugs struck her in the head with a gun. She slipped into unconsciousness, but not before feeling the blows and kicks to her body.

Family members found her sprawled on the sidewalk, bleeding, bruised, and unresponsive. They rushed her to the hospital to be treated. Days later she woke up, initially unable to move her legs and feet. For nearly a week, doctors tended to her injuries.

Police remove anti-government protesters from the "United for Freedom" march on October 14, 2018, in Managua, Nicaragua. Political upheaval forces many people to seek refuge in other countries.

Wet Foot/Dry Foot Policy

Cuba, an island nation in the Caribbean, lies only 90 miles (145 km) from the US border, separated by the Straits of Florida. For years, many Cubans risked crossing the waterway in small boats because of a US policy known informally as "wet foot/dry foot." It meant that once Cuban citizens stepped onto American soil ("dry foot"), they automatically received asylum. But if they were intercepted by US authorities before they reached US shores ("wet foot") they were sent back to Cuba or to another country. This policy began in 1995 under President Bill Clinton.

But in 2017, based on changing relations between the US and Cuban governments, President Barack Obama reversed this protection for Cuban migrants. From then on, those seeking asylum would need to follow the same procedures as migrants from other countries. If they did not meet the requirements for asylum, they could be sent back. Cubans would no longer enjoy a preferred status in the immigration system.

While recovering, she learned that her shop had been ransacked and robbed. They took everything—everything she had worked so hard to build for herself and her son. All of this happened because she had stood up and marched in protest.

"When they attacked me, they didn't do it with the intention of frightening me, but rather of killing me, of leaving one more voice in silence,"[5] said Bárbara. Some members of her own family grew distant because they feared the government. So, Bárbara moved from one loyal family member's house to another while recovering her strength. She hoped to remain hidden. An aunt, who lived in Miami, Florida, offered to take Bárbara in. But what about her son? Could she take him too? Could she leave him behind? Would the United States believe her story and offer her asylum? Did she have enough evidence to make her case? There were no clear answers.

Fitero: Natural Disaster and Poverty

Others who seek asylum are escaping the chaos and devastation wreaked by natural disasters. This was the case for Fitero

This tent city in Port-au-Prince, Haiti, is one of many that sprung up in the wake of a devastating earthquake that occurred in January 2010. People left homeless by the quake built makeshift shelters from cardboard, sheet metal, blankets, and other material.

Janvier, whose situation at home in Haiti had finally hit a crisis point. In January 2010, this severely impoverished country experienced a 7.0 magnitude earthquake. It killed more than 250,000 people, left 1.5 million homeless, and made life in the island nation unbearable. Hospitals were overwhelmed, infrastructure was destroyed, disease and hunger were rampant, and lack of clean water and electricity left Haitians desperate.

Fitero left Haiti in 2014 and followed a mass migration to South America—specifically to Brazil. He knew that Brazil had many construction jobs because it was hosting the World Cup and the upcoming 2016 Summer Olympics. The country also offered humanitarian visas to Haitians in response to the horrific living conditions on their island. Brazilian officials encouraged migrants to seek asylum.

Fitero's new residence also had problems, however. Jobs dried up after the Olympics, and the economy slowed. Anti-immigrant sentiment spread throughout the country after the election of President Jair Bolsonaro. Haitian immigrants also faced racial discrimination because they were of Black African descent. Thus, Fitero continued on, this time to Chile.

Initially, Fitero found work; he also got married and started a family. But no matter how hard they tried, Fitero and his wife struggled to survive. Extreme poverty, discrimination, and difficulties getting residency paperwork forced the Janvier family to leave and seek asylum in the United States. From Chile, they would need to travel through Bolivia, Peru, Ecuador, Colombia, Central America, and Mexico. But the couple agreed that they could no longer stay, so they took the risk and headed north with their young son.

Danelia: Violence Against Women

Gender-based violence—which includes sexual assault, partner violence, and family and spousal abuse—is another reason why people leave their countries to seek asylum elsewhere. In the Central American country of El Salvador, for example, a woman dies of gender-based violence every twenty-four hours; the United Nations reports that 67 percent of Salvadoran women have suffered some sort of violence. One of these women is Danelia Silva, and gender-based violence is what drove her to seek asylum.

From the age of fifteen, Danelia had to fend for herself. Both of her parents fled to the United States in order to make money to support their children. They left Danelia in charge of raising her younger brother. Money arrived each month—as much as her parents could afford to send. After a few years they had saved enough to send for their son, but they did not have enough for Danelia too. She remained in El Salvador alone.

At age eighteen, she gave birth to her daughter Sara. Soon after, she and her boyfriend, Carlos, added to the family with another daughter, Natalia, and a son, Javier. Shortly after Javier arrived, things changed. Carlos verbally abused Danelia in front of the children and others. He did not allow her to speak to others, especially not men. If a man spoke to her, she would pay the price

Gangs

Throughout Central America, neighborhoods are often controlled by gangs. They demand shelter, transportation, information, or payment for protection. Gangs steal personal property or force people to hide drugs or engage in illegal activities. Members force youth to join their ranks or face death. Their violent behavior causes citizens to flee to the United States and seek asylum. But the irony is that these gangs originated in America.

As El Salvador erupted in civil war during the 1980s, hundreds of thousands of people fled the war-torn nation, many settling into the neighborhoods of Los Angeles, California. As displaced youth sought to connect with others, they formed gangs for protection, identity, and income. But illegal actions sent many to jail, where the gang culture continued. As more crimes were committed by gang members, the United States sent thousands back to their homelands. When they returned to places such as El Salvador, they found their country ripped apart by war and no way to make a living. The gangs grew stronger and more violent, and corrupt governments allowed them to flourish. Gang violence remains one of the main reasons asylum seekers flee to the US southern border.

when they got home. "Carlos would grab me, throw me to the floor, and kick me over and over. He hit me a lot," says Danelia. "One time he grabbed a baseball bat and hit me. He hit my entire right side with it."[6]

Her children witnessed the attacks and started to imitate what they saw. Her daughter hit and kicked her doll and pulled its hair. The children screamed and swore at friends. Danelia knew she could no longer stay with Carlos. For her children's sake, and to save her own life, she fled to a friend's house. But her partner tracked them down. Again and again she tried to run away.

Carlos finally agreed to let her go, but with one condition. She must leave Javier behind. It broke Danelia's heart to leave her son. But she knew if she stayed, she would probably die at Carlos's hands. At least she and her daughters could get away. She hoped they could reunite with her parents in Texas.

At a friend's house, she and the girls prepared to leave. That is when Danelia received a visit from Carlos's sister. She had brought along an unexpected surprise: Javier. It felt like a miracle to Danelia to have all three of her children together. She did not waste a minute. After throwing one change of clothes for each of them in a bag, she and the children left. Using money that her mother had sent to her online, they grabbed the next bus from San Salvador and headed for the border, where she hoped to seek asylum. Danelia did not have much of a plan and very little money. But what she did have were her children, family in the United States, and hope that they could somehow make their way to a new life.

Adrian: Gang Violence

The terror of gang violence is widespread throughout Central America. It sends people like Adrian Cruz fleeing for their lives, with the hope of finding asylum in the United States. Adrian grew up in a gang-controlled barrio in Guatemala City. His mother owned a small shop in this dangerous district selling kitchen goods. That is how this single mother supported her son.

Members of a local gang made their rounds throughout town demanding money from store owners. If they paid, they were left alone. Adrian remembered the day when an intruder asked his mother for money. She did not have enough, but she asked if maybe she could pay a part of what they wanted. The man did not answer. Instead, he pulled out a gun, shot her to death, and walked away. Five-year-old Adrian witnessed it all.

Soon after, he moved in with his grandparents, who cared for Adrian and three other cousins. They sent the children to school and provided food and clothing for them. Adrian eventually lost interest in school and began working as a painter. When he turned seventeen, things took a turn for the worse.

Gang members, many of whom Adrian knew from the town, wanted him to join. "If you don't join, we'll kill you,"[7] they threatened.

> "If you don't join, we'll kill you."[7]
>
> —Adrian Cruz, asylum seeker

The wife of a murdered bus driver cries at the crime scene in Guatemala City in December 2008. Criminal gangs killed nearly 160 bus drivers in Guatemala that year alone.

They needed more recruits to sell drugs and demand protection money. "I don't want to join this gang with you,"[8] Adrian recalled saying.

One night, outside his home, they attacked him. "They had guns, and one had a knife as long as my forearm. I knew the guy with the knife. . . . He was a little guy called 'the Rat,'"[9] recalled Adrian. Gang members shot him twice, and the Rat slit Adrian's throat. The gang members ran away, leaving their victim for dead.

But Adrian did not die. Emergency vehicles arrived and transported him to the hospital, where he recovered. Soon the gang heard the news, and Adrian knew his life remained in danger. He hid for several months, regaining his strength, and then he told his grandparents that he planned to leave.

"Why do you have to leave? We don't know what's going to happen to you. It's very dangerous on the road,"[10] his grandmother had said. But Adrian felt he had no choice. He slipped out of town secretly, without saying good-bye to his family. He called them from the road when he was safely on his way: "I'm going to see if God lets me make it to the United States."[11] His grand-mother had pleaded with him to stay: "And when you arrive, you will not have family there. Don't go."[12]

Maureny: Intellectual and Academic Censorship

Another reason people seek asylum is to escape persecution and censorship. That is why Maureny Reves Benitez and her family left Cuba. In an effort to manage information provided to its citizens, the Cuban government maintains control over all print and other media. This censorship suppresses words, images, or ideas that are politically offensive. That is the world in which Maureny's father, Yanko Reves, worked as a university English professor.

The government branded Yanko a critic of the island's government. His wife, Anisleydis Benitez, explained that "he was persecuted for thinking differently."[13] Yanko and others who speak out are subject to harassment, violence, detention, travel restrictions, and raids on their homes and offices. The United Nations High Commissioner for Refugees (UNHCR) granted him refugee status in 2015 because his life was in danger. That is when he left his homeland to relocate to Trinidad and Tobago—an island nation near the South American country of Venezuela. He also left behind Anisleydis and his thirteen-year-old daughter, Maureny.

For nearly two years, the mother and daughter waited to receive the same protection from the UNHCR and finally joined Yanko in Trinidad and Tobago. The islands promised work and travel documents, along with public assistance and medical care to refugees. But it did not happen. The family requested that their status be transferred to another country where things might be

> "He was persecuted for thinking differently."[13]
>
> —Anisleydis Benitez, asylum seeker

better. The organization refused, and that is when the family decided to immigrate to the United States.

But first they needed to reach the Venezuelan mainland. In the middle of the night, Maureny, Anisleydis, and Yanko boarded a broken-down boat with twenty-seven other migrants. For six hours, they endured high seas. Maureny broke into tears, afraid of what might happen. Then she remembered a hymn that her grandmother (*abuela*) used to sing to calm her. "When I started singing, everyone on the boat started singing along—some of them didn't know the words, but they sang anyway. . . . Just like that, the current weakened."[14] Maureny believed it was a miracle sent from her *abuela*. They safely stepped ashore in Venezuela, but their journey had just begun.

The Asylum Process

The UNHCR has declared that "seeking asylum is a fundamental human right. Everyone has the right to life and liberty. Everyone has the right to freedom from fear. Everyone has the right to seek asylum from persecution."[15] But these ideals are not always borne out in national laws, which can change depending on who is in charge of a country.

> "Seeking asylum is a fundamental human right."[15]
>
> —United Nations High Commissioner for Refugees

In 2018, for example, US attorney general Jeff Sessions abruptly changed the criteria for those seeking asylum. "Generally, claims by aliens pertaining to domestic violence or gang violence perpetrated by nongovernmental actors will not qualify for asylum,"[16] he stated. He argued that the United States should not be held responsible for another country's inability to control crime. This decision, which was supported by then-president Donald Trump, allowed US Customs and Border Protection (CBP) officers to turn away anyone seeking asylum whose claim dealt with violence caused by anyone other than government personnel. The Trump administration effectively overturned decades of asylum protocol and sent countless victims back to their countries to face renewed violence and retribution from their attackers.

However, in 2021, the new attorney general under President Biden, Merrick Garland, reinstated protection for victims of domestic and gang violence. In doing so, he recognized the right of those seeking asylum to make their case. This humanitarian ruling supports those who are forced to flee their countries because of these abuses. Still, not everyone who seeks asylum is granted it.

CHAPTER TWO

The Journeys

The most physically dangerous part of the asylum-seeking process is the journey. Each path to the southern border of the United States is different, and many factors contribute to the difficulty those seeking asylum face. Some travel with young children, and others hit the road on their own. Geography can play a significant part in the experience, depending on the path taken. Mountains, jungles, and deserts all present significant obstacles to weary travelers. Finances also add to the struggle. They need enough money to pay for buses, guides, lodging, and food over weeks and sometimes months on the road. Travelers also encounter robbers, and physical violence, and otherwise put their lives at risk as they move north.

Bárbara: Remain in Mexico

Nearly one year after Bárbara survived the attack outside her store in Nicaragua, she made the difficult decision to leave her home and seek asylum in the United States. Unsure whether she would be able to keep her son safe as they traveled, Bárbara decided to go alone, with a promise to her son that they would reunite in the United States soon. She leaned over her sleeping son and softly kissed him good-bye. "Fue el peor momento de mi vida,"[17] recalled Bárbara. In English: *It was the worst moment of my life.*

She left before dawn one morning in May and headed toward Honduras. She snuck out of town on foot and then traveled by car, bus, horseback, and truck through the mountains. Because of her involvement in the political protests, she knew the government would not permit her to leave. Her passport had been flagged on "la lista negra"[18]—the black list. Like many, Bárbara paid a guide to accompany her along the way. Known as *coyotes*, these individuals smuggle people across the border. But somewhere on her trek, the escort abandoned her, forcing her to find and pay for another one.

She traveled on through Guatemala and Belize before crossing the Mexican border. A robber held her at gunpoint, demanding all her valuables. Bárbara surrendered everything but the items she needed the most—her documents. Armed with photos, notes, hospital records, and statements from witnesses, Bárbara hoped these papers would prove that she suffered persecution at the hands of the Nicaraguan government. They held the key to her asylum case. She negotiated with the bandit to keep them. A stranger let her borrow a phone to call her family for help. Someone wired her more money to keep her alive on the final part of the journey. She reached the US border at San Diego in June, just days before her twenty-ninth birthday. She had made it.

But when she asked for asylum, officers slapped handcuffs on her and took her into custody. As a single adult crossing the border, she learned that she must wait in Mexico until her asylum case came up. This was due to something called the Migrant Protection Protocols (MPP), also known as "Remain in Mexico." Under this policy, people seeking to enter the United States from Mexico, either illegally or without proper documentation, may be returned to Mexico to wait while their cases are processed.

The MPP policy was established in early 2019 under President Trump. According to the Refugee and Immigrant Center for Education and Legal Services (RAICES), "Remain in Mexico . . . has become an invisible wall at the border, effectively ending asylum. Since it began in January 2019, only 0.8% of asylum seekers in Migrant Protection Protocols have been granted asylum."[19] In other words, less than 1 percent of those returned to Mexico have successfully made their case for asylum. President Biden

Migrants from Central America, sent back to Mexico to await the outcome of their cases under the Migrant Protection Protocols (MPP), eat at El Buen Pastor shelter in Ciudad Juarez, Mexico, on February 28, 2020.

amended the policy in the early days of his administration, but Bárbara did not count among the unaccompanied minors, single mothers with children, pregnant women, or those with severe health issues who, under the policy, are allowed to stay in the United States. Thus, officials walked Bárbara back across the border to Tijuana, Mexico. Her first court hearing was scheduled to be held in 158 days, meaning she would need to remain in Mexico for at least five months.

Bárbara managed to find an apartment in a very poor neighborhood. She worked as a waitress and talked with her son every day by phone. Bárbara carried on with her life, waiting for her hearing, hoping that one day she would be granted asylum and be able to send for her son to join her.

Danelia: Single Mother

Fleeing for one's life is difficult enough. But for single mothers, the challenges of this dangerous journey are compounded by being responsible for their children. Danelia left Nicaragua with her three young children knowing it would be treacherous, but she believed she had no choice. Danelia's mother continued transferring money to her online—$50 here, $100 there. With her kids in tow, Danelia spent most of what she received on food, water, hotels, and transportation. When they reached the Guatemalan border, guards charged them $150 to cross the Rio Paz—Peace River. But the conditions there were anything but calm. "The current was strong, and the rocks hurt a lot," says Danelia. "But you have to do it because you can't cross in your shoes. This was the most difficult part of crossing that border."[20] People slipped and fell. The rushing water pushed some over. But with the help of strangers, Danelia and the children made it safely to the other side.

Her parents hired a *coyote* to help them with the rest of the journey. The man charged them a total of $14,000 to make it to the US border and to pay for transportation and motels. The money would also be used to bribe police and gang members to allow Danelia and her family to cross their territory. The *coyote* received a first payment of $4,000, but shortly thereafter, he abandoned them at a bus station in southern Mexico. With no money, Danelia and her children spent the night in the terminal. They had no dinner that night, nor breakfast the next morning.

> "The current was strong, and the rocks hurt a lot. But you have to do it because you can't cross in your shoes. This was the most difficult part of crossing that border."[20]
>
> —Danelia Silva, asylum seeker

Immigration police were patrolling the station. If caught, Danelia and her children would immediately be sent home. Luckily, a restaurant worker warned her about the immigration police and helped her find a place to stay at a nearby shelter. She found herself surrounded by other mothers traveling with their children. After waiting there for some time, Danelia met up with some family members who lived in Mexico. They drove Danelia and her children to the border, where Danelia turned herself over to CBP.

Feeding Hungry Stowaways

Asylum seekers riding La Bestia (the train route through Mexico to the US border) are always wondering where they will find their next meal. Since 1995, a group of women in La Patrona, Mexico, have tried to help where they can. It began when two sisters waiting at a train crossing heard shouts from the top of passing freight cars, pleading for food. The girls pulled bread and milk from their grocery bags and threw them up to the riders. That is how a tradition began.

Decades later, the women of this tiny town continue the routine. Known as Las Patronas, these women feed the train riders who pass through their village. Local businesses donate the food, then the women prepare large cauldrons of rice and beans and make hundreds of tortillas to share. Ten tortillas, along with portions of cooked rice and beans, are packed into baggies and are then tied up in plastic grocery bags. As the train slows and whistles its approach, the women race to the tracks with their bags. They fling them high into the air to the rooftops of the train. Some women hold them out to the outstretched arms of riders clinging to the ladders on the side of each car. Although these volunteers are named after their town, in Spanish the word *patrona* means "patron saint." For those stowaways on La Bestia, these women are truly that.

She presented copies of emails and Facebook postings that Carlos had written as evidence of the death threats and harassment she faced. Because she was traveling with small children, the officers admitted her to the United States; under the MPP, single mothers with children, along with unaccompanied minors, pregnant women, and those with severe health issues are allowed to stay in the United States as they await their hearings. They issued her a notice to appear in immigration court for a final ruling on her asylum case. Meanwhile, a local priest sponsored them and helped transport them to Danelia's parents' home in Texas. This joyful event marked the first time Sara, Natalia, and Javier met their grandparents. It also began a new chapter in their lives. Danelia found work, and her children returned to school. Although they still have hurdles to overcome while waiting for asylum, they no longer live in fear of domestic and gender-based violence.

Maureny: Crossing Terrains

Depending on the asylum seeker's path to the border, geography can add even more peril to a journey. Mountains, jungles, deserts, and bodies of water all present unexpected challenges.

With their dangerous ocean journey behind them, Maureny and her family believed they were safe. But Venezuelan authorities, under the influence of a violent and corrupt government, subjected the migrants to a strip search. Her mother had been prepared for this and had sewn their money into bras and had hidden some of it in their feminine pads. But the agents knew all the tricks. "They took everything from us, they even took our food,"[21] says Maureny.

Still, they managed to move on. The Darién Gap, which is 60 miles (97 km) of dense jungle that spans the Colombia-Panama border, came next. The only way through is on foot. Maureny recalls, "My dad told me to look straight and to keep walking. He said nothing bad would happen to me because he was there to protect me."[22] She was unprepared for the conditions. They traveled beneath the thick jungle canopy for days. Torrential rains, rugged mountain paths, rushing rivers, and venomous snakes all threatened their lives. In the middle of the trek, an important date arrived: Maureny's seventeenth birthday. She cried, thinking of her birthdays back in Cuba. She never could have imagined how she would spend this one. But her group of fellow travelers surprised her at midnight and sang to her as they continued hiking through the jungle.

For days they walked, and nearing the end of that part of the journey, robbers struck once again. With no food or water, they feared the worst. But they prevailed and eventually made it to Bajo Chiquito, Panama, a welcome point for migrants who complete their trek through the jungle.

> "My dad told me to look straight and to keep walking. He said nothing bad would happen to me because he was there to protect me."[22]
>
> —Maureny Reves Benitez, asylum seeker

25

Two Honduran mothers and their children rest after being taken into custody by Border Patrol agents after crossing the Rio Grande River into the United States illegally.

In a nearby village, Maureny and her parents presented their visas, passports, and other documentation. The process next involved taking photographs, fingerprinting all ten fingers, and conducting a retinal scan. All of this data was then registered by the Biometric Identification Transnational Migration Alert Program (BITMAP). This US-designed program tracks the movements of migrants through other countries as they make their way to the US border. It also allows authorities to control the number of people admitted on any given day. After nearly a month in Panama, the family moved northward to Mexico.

The Mexican government offered them humanitarian visas. That ensured that they could travel throughout the country. They finally made their way to the Mexican city of San Luis Rio Colorado. They added their names to a list of more than fifteen hundred others and waited to apply for asylum.

Number 929—that was the number given to Maureny and her parents the day they arrived. For nearly five months, they remained in Mexico. Her parents found work at a local restaurant to make ends meet as they waited. Finally, their number came up, and CBP officers processed their paperwork and transported them to Phoenix, Arizona. They boarded a plane at Phoenix Sky Harbor International Airport destined for Miami, Florida, where family sponsors awaited their arrival.

Maureny and her parents entered the country with proper paperwork and visas, filed an asylum application, and completed an interview with US Citizenship and Immigration Services. However, due to a considerable backlog in the immigration courts, it might take up to three years before the family receives a decision about their asylum case.

Adrian: Unaccompanied Minor

Seventeen-year-old Adrian knew he had to leave Guatamala or else the gangs would find him again. So, he set out alone, hoping the United States would grant him asylum. Little did this unaccompanied minor know that he would share the journey with countless other young people on that same quest.

Adrian boarded a bus for the Guatemala-Mexico border. He had no documents with him. When he learned that the immigration officers refused entry to anyone without proper paperwork, he knew they would send him home. But fellow travelers explained a scheme to Adrian to beat the system, and it worked.

A few miles before the immigration stop, Adrian got off the bus. He walked into the nearby hills, skirted the station, then reemerged on the Mexican side of the same road. He then boarded the bus farther up the road for the next part of the journey.

When he arrived in Arriaga, Chiapas, Adrian changed his form of transportation, hopping aboard freight trains known as La Bestia ("the Beast"). The freight trains earned that name because of the danger involved in riding them. As the trains pass by, hitchhikers jump aboard and climb up to the top of the cars. But not everyone makes it. Some fall beneath the train, where they are either maimed or killed.

Technology on the Road

Besides money and documents, asylum seekers need information as they travel. Almost all who make the journey carry a smartphone, which serves as a lifeline to valuable information. Travelers use their smartphones to stay in touch with loved ones at home and abroad. Phones are also used to access social media, get news, share a traveler's whereabouts, and learn which routes to avoid or use.

But social media also spreads misinformation. Facts can be distorted, which is especially problematic when it influences the movement of asylum seekers. For example, some US immigration policies changed when Joe Biden became president in 2021, including one that opened the door to a limited number of asylum seekers. But social media became flooded with stories that seemed to indicate the border had been reopened to everyone. This led those seeking asylum to flock to the US southern border under false pretenses: the United States had *not* reopened the border to all asylum seekers. As a result, some were detained, and many others were deported.

"While I was traveling, I made a few friends. We'd all help each other," says Adrian. He and his travel mates rode along, clinging to anything for safety. Rickety tracks and sharp curves could easily throw a rider from the rooftop of the freight trains. "We'd go through tunnels and have to tuck in and stay low. I did see accidents. . . . Some people get hurt and some die that way,"[23] Adrian explains. They watched for low-hanging branches on trees that could sweep a dozing passenger from his perch. But those he traveled with looked out for one another, keeping an eye out for bandits that sometimes boarded at train stations in order to rob riders.

A volunteer group known as Las Betas works to offer assistance and aid to travelers at train stops. They call for the ambulance if someone is hurt. They give first aid supplies, food, and water. Traveling at night through the desert is very cold, and riders have little protec-

> "We'd go through tunnels and have to tuck in and stay low. I did see accidents."[23]
>
> —Adrian Cruz, asylum seeker

tion; Las Betas gives them blankets, hoodies, and sweatshirts—anything to ease the discomfort of the long trip.

People's generosity in sharing what little they had amazed Adrian. *Casas del migrantes* ("migrant houses"), offered him the most comfort on his journey. These houses, located in every Mexican state, opened their doors to those passing through, offering food, clothing, and a place to stay for a few days.

Adrian finally made it to the border, but Mexican authorities nabbed him before he crossed. Mexican officials immediately deported Adrian to Guatemala, where he had begun his journey.

Migrants cling to the freight train known as "La Bestia" while locals hand them food and water for their journey. Many people who are seeking a better life are killed traveling this way.

Five days later, he left again. He would not give up. After another series of dangerous train rides, robberies, and months on the road, Adrian reached the border at Mexicali-Calexico. He tried to sneak across, but agents caught him. However, because he made it onto US soil, he was allowed to stay and be sent to a detention center; that is because US law protects unaccompanied minors. Adrian had no paperwork to make his asylum case. But the evidence could be found on his body—a long scar across his neck and bullet wounds in his ribcage. He hoped it would be enough.

Reaching Their Destinations

With their journeys behind them, people seeking asylum face renewed anxiety at the border. Will they be able to stay and make their case? Do they have the proper paperwork? Can they remain in the United States? With language barriers, diminished finances, and often a lack of legal help, these people face even more obstacles once they arrive. Whether crossing at a port of entry or illegally entering between checkpoints, a migrant's journey is far from over. Unknown hurdles and long waits can remain in their quest for asylum.

CHAPTER THREE

At the Border

For many, arriving at the border seems like the end of the quest. Historically, when asylum seekers reached the United States, CBP would detain them, process their identification documents, and run security checks. An asylum officer would conduct a credible fear interview. If the asylum seeker established that he or she had been persecuted, or there was a significant possibility they would be harmed if deported, the officer would issue a notice to appear. This document granted the person a hearing before an immigration judge, where asylum could be granted or denied. While waiting for this to occur, asylum seekers could be placed on parole, which allowed the individual to be temporarily released in the United States. Family members or sponsors would take asylum seekers in while waiting for the immigration process to move forward.

However, ever-shifting immigration policies have complicated the process and contributed to delays, detentions, and denials. Inadequate documentation can derail the process. Language barriers and lack of legal representation contribute to the misunderstanding of rights. In March 2020, a public health order known as Title 42 allowed for the quick expulsion of asylum seekers in response to the COVID-19 pandemic. Out of concern over the virus, these people never had the chance to apply for asylum. With the threat of deportation looming over the new arrivals, their next steps in the asylum process presented a continuation of their difficult journey.

Asylum Seekers Processed

Many asylum seekers cross the border at ports of entry to lawfully enter the United States. Others choose to cross illegally. Travelers who cross this way can still seek asylum by turning themselves over to the US Border Patrol agents.

Emilia is one asylum seeker who went the latter route. Around 2019, she and her daughter, Lauda, fled violence in Honduras and made the choice to enter the United States illegally, with a group of about two dozen other travelers. But there were no patrols around when they arrived. With nearly 2,000 miles (3,219 km) of border, it is difficult to monitor all of the crossings. With water and provisions gone, the group wondered how long they would wait. Border Patrol agents finally arrived. After checking identification cards and birth certificates, they loaded the migrants into buses headed for a Border Patrol processing facility.

Once they arrived at the center, workers passed out sandwiches, juice, and cookies; employees checked identification and paperwork again. Next came fingerprinting and examining any other data from previous border crossings. This security check prevents any asylum seeker with a criminal record from being considered.

While Emilia and her daughter waited for clearance, personnel moved them to a small, very cold room. Many refer to these holding cells as *las hieleras*, which is Spanish for "ice boxes." The typical holding room contains a single toilet and a drinking fountain. Some cells have thin mats for sleeping, but often, nothing cushions detainees from the cold, hard concrete floor. Emilia received a flimsy aluminum "blanket," meant to keep body heat in and cold out. As the day wore on, more people squeezed in, at times so tightly that only some could lie on the floor to sleep. Others sat nearby waiting for their turns to stretch out and rest.

Emilia and the other detainees could not tell whether it was day or night. There were no windows, and lights remained on twenty-four hours a day. Breakfast was the only indication that a new day had dawned. For three days, Emilia and Lauda waited.

Migrants from Colombia stand in front of a wall that marks the border between Mexico and the United States. This group is waiting to be processed after turning themselves over to authorities on May 12, 2021, in Yuma, Arizona.

Next, Emilia was put through what is known as the credible fear interview. During this meeting, Emilia shared her story with the official. She told of violence that included an attack on her neighbor by local gang members. They beat him and threw rocks at his head, leaving him bleeding in the street, because he had no money to pay for protection. Emilia feared for her life because she had witnessed the attack. "It was horrible that I couldn't do anything about it. Fortunately, he lived—but the truth is if you try to stop something like this, they'll just do the same to you," she explained. "All you can do in Honduras is shut your mouth, because nobody is safe there."[24]

Upon passing the interview, Emilia and Lauda were transported to a shelter run by the International Rescue Committee in Phoenix. The staff

> "The truth is if you try to stop something like this, they'll just do the same to you. All you can do in Honduras is shut your mouth, because nobody is safe there."[24]
>
> —Emilia, asylum seeker

Affirmative vs. Defensive Asylum

There are two paths to claiming asylum: the affirmative asylum process and the defensive asylum process. Those seeking asylum who have proper identification, enter at a port of entry, and pass a credible fear interview qualify for the affirmative asylum process. Even those who enter the country illegally, with proper identification and evidence of persecution, may meet the criteria. Those migrants who have prior immigration violations, lack identification, or are ordered to be deported but pass a credible fear interview may still apply for asylum through the defensive asylum process. Both types of asylum seekers must complete and submit paperwork within one year of entry. Cases are decided in front of one of the five hundred immigration judges who currently serve in this position. In 2021, US Citizenship and Immigration Services had a backlog of over 1.3 million immigration cases. Nearly 400,000 of them are affirmative asylum cases.

welcomed them with hugs and cheers. Emilia and her daughter both cried. The shelter provided a doctor and good food. There was soap and feminine supplies, along with diapers, clothes, and toys. "We could feel the love and concern,"[25] says Emilia.

Volunteers provided guidance to the young mother and her daughter to prepare for the next steps in the asylum process. Having passed the credible fear interview, Emilia received a notice to appear. Those at the shelter also helped her make travel arrangements to meet up with family in Texas, as she waited to appear before the immigration judge.

Asylum Seekers Separated

Another mother from Central America had a much more traumatic experience. Andrea and her three-year-old son, José, escaped a gang who beat her and threatened to kill her. She and José spent weeks on the road riding buses, walking, and taking a boat before reaching the US border in Rio Grande City, Texas. Andrea had done everything the "right" way. She crossed at a legal port of entry. She provided identification documents. She had a family sponsor in New Jersey who offered to shelter them. Things should have gone smoothly, but they did not.

For three days, the two spent time at a processing center in Texas. She told her story to the agents, but she still needed to pass the credible fear interview. In the meantime, she and her son needed to remain in detention, but that would happen at another facility.

Andrea thought they would go together. Instead, the immigration official ordered her to place José in the back of a truck. That is when she realized she would not be joining him. This was because in 2018, under President Trump, it became common practice to separate children from their parents at the border as a way to deter immigrants from coming to the United States. "He cried and scrambled to get back to [me] as the vehicle drove away,"[26] recalls Andrea.

For six weeks, she endured crowded conditions at the new detention center. Packed fifty to a room, she and the other women slept in bunk beds and lived like prisoners. There was no privacy, not even to shower. All the while she worried about José and where he was.

Andrea's attorney explained that they likely transported him to a tender-age shelter out east. *Tender age* refers to children under the age of five. With her lawyer's help, Andrea tracked him down. The mother and son talked by phone, but José often cried while they talked. Both José and Andrea suffered from depression, headaches, fear, helplessness, crying, trouble eating, and difficulty sleeping.

After forty-one days, authorities released Andrea, giving her permission to stay and work in the United States while she waited for the backlog of asylum cases to clear the courts. She flew immediately to New York to be reunited with her son. "I was very happy to see him. But for José, it was very hard for him. He didn't want to be near me. He wouldn't listen to me,"[27] she says. Her son blamed her for their separation.

In those early months, living with family in New Jersey, José clung to his mother. She could not be out of his sight without him asking where she was going. He begged her not to leave the house. Kathy Hirsh-Pasek, a senior fellow with the Brookings Institution, uses the term "toxic shock" to describe what family separation does to children and parents. "The trauma that many of these parents and children are experiencing on American soil threatens to undermine their future development. . . . The impact on their bodies and minds can last a lifetime."[28]

Despite this tragedy, Andrea and José are considered lucky. "Since July 1, 2017, more than 5,000 migrating children have been taken from their parents and some still are awaiting reunifi-

Illegal migrants sit in cages in an immigration detention facility in McAllen, Texas, on June 17, 2018. Many parents were separated from their children.

cation,"[29] explains Catherine Weiss, a partner at the law firm of Lowenstein Sandler. The government eventually discontinued the policy of separating parents from their children at the border. But due to a failure to keep accurate records, the search continues to locate children and reunite them with their parents.

> "Since July 1, 2017, more than 5,000 migrating children have been taken from their parents and some still are awaiting reunification."[29]
>
> —Catherine Weiss, attorney

Asylum Seekers Detained

According to the Department of Homeland Security, US authorities have taken more than 445,000 unaccompanied minors into custody along the southern border since 2013. Unaccompanied minors, or children under age eighteen who are traveling alone, receive special treatment at the US border. Whether they cross at a port of entry or illegally, they will not be expelled. Children are usually taken into custody by CBP, but those detentions are limited in length and must meet certain requirements.

This is why when ten-year-old Ariany crossed the US border alone, CBP did not deport her but instead sent her to the Donna Camp in Texas. This detention should have lasted less than seventy-two hours. However, Ariany spent more than three weeks there, in an overcrowded plastic cubicle. Children from toddlers to teens shared the space. "We were very cold," says Ariany. "We had nowhere to sleep so we shared mats. We were five girls on two mats."[30] She and other girls interviewed complained about rotten food, wet conditions due to dripping pipes, and head lice. At most, the girls showered once a week and rarely saw daylight, unless lined up outside waiting for meals to be served. "We all cried, from the youngest up. There were two-year-old babies crying because they wanted their mother,"[31] recalls Cindy, another detainee. The older girls tried to comfort the littler ones.

According to a 1997 US Supreme Court decision, immigration officials must "give detained minors a certain quality of life, including things such as food, drinking water, medical assistance in emergencies, toilets, sinks, temperature control, supervision, and as much separation from unrelated adults as possible."[32] Clearly, the conditions at facilities like the Donna Camp fail to meet such criteria.

After weeks of waiting, officials released Ariany to her mother. It is unclear why it took so long to do so. By law, unaccompanied minors should be transferred to the Office of Refugee Resettlement (ORR) as quickly as possible. ORR's job is to move these children into the care of family members living in the United States. For those who lack an immediate family member in the states, minors are placed into temporary shelters until a vetted sponsor can be found. Foster care is another option for children who do not have family members or friends to care for them.

The unprecedented numbers of unaccompanied minors at the border has strained the system, causing additional trauma to children. Delays in reunification with family members; overcrowded, prison-like living conditions; and the lack of care for basic needs cause these youngest asylum seekers to suffer both physically and mentally.

Asylum Seekers Trapped

Many seeking asylum believe that once they cross the border and are taken into custody, they are on their way to claiming asylum in the United States. But this is not necessarily the case, as a Nicaraguan man named Cesar learned. Cesar and his family left Nicaragua because of political unrest and threats to his life by the paramilitary. After enduring weeks of dangerous travel, the former taxi driver—along with his wife, Carolina, and their nine-year-old son, Donovan—made it across the southern border. "We saw the officers in green and we felt protected," he said. "For the first time since these problems started, we felt protected."[33]

Zero Tolerance Leads to Family Separation

In May 2018, the Trump administration enacted a zero-tolerance approach to anyone caught crossing the border illegally. Immigrants who crossed between ports of entry would be apprehended and detained without inspection. This included any asylum seekers, preventing them from making their case to CBP agents. Initially, adults with children would be held in family detention centers. But because children could not remain in those facilities for more than twenty days, the government removed them from their parents and treated them as unaccompanied minors. Authorities transferred them to the US Department of Health and Human Services for care and custody. They sent those children to youth detention centers, group homes, or into the foster care system across the country. The zero-tolerance policy directly resulted in the separation of more than five thousand children from their parents. Inadequate records of the whereabouts of these minors prevented reunification of families even after the policy ended in 2018. More than three years later, there are roughly fifteen hundred children who remain separated from their parents.

Cesar and his family experienced the typical screening at the immigration center—fingerprints, photographs, documentation, holding rooms. After the interviewer listened to the family's experience with violence, he determined that they met the credible fear criteria. They received a court date to plead their case before a judge. Cesar felt relief, but not for long.

That is because the MPP policy determined what came next. Cesar and his family did not count among the groups that are exempt from remaining in Mexico—unaccompanied minors, single mothers with children, pregnant women, or those with severe health issues. Therefore, the US government sent Cesar, Carolina, and Donovan back across the border to await their next hearing. According to the Transactional Records Access Clearinghouse, a nonprofit and nonpartisan research center at Syracuse University, authorities returned more than seventy thousand men, women, and children from 2019 to 2021. Cesar's family ended up in Ciudad Juárez, one of the most dangerous towns along the US–Mexico border. This is also a typical experience; according to RAICES, "Many of the areas MPP delivered migrants to are places with the highest level of travel warnings for US citizens."[34]

Under pressure from the United States, the Mexican government agreed to provide resources for those waiting for their court appearances. Mexico quickly became overwhelmed by the sheer number of people waiting. With shelters full, makeshift refugee camps sprang up, but conditions soon deteriorated—there was no medical care, poor sanitation, lack of food, no work, and no educational services for children. To add to the agony, organized crime and drug cartels control many border cities, where kidnappings, robberies, violence, and murders frequently occur. Cesar feared for his loved ones and felt trapped because he could not return to his home. Instead, they waited in Mexico with their lives at risk and no family or friends nearby to help.

Asylum Seekers Assisted

In response to the conditions on the southern side of the US border, some organizations offer relief to those forced to wait. For example, the International Organization for Migration, which is part of the United Nations, distributes debit cards of $800.00 every two weeks for a family of four. Private organizations have set up daily classes for children who are awaiting the process, and American attorneys offer support to those in need.

Behind a tall concrete wall in Reynosa, Mexico, sits Senda de Vida ("Path of Life"). This 10-acre (4 ha) riverbank migrant camp holds more than twelve hundred migrants on any given day. Another fifteen hundred wait outside the complex for room to open up. They are here because they have been placed on waiting lists. Many of them seek asylum. While waiting for their turns at Senda de Vida, Pastor Hector De Luna oversees a process that is organized, fair, and relatively inexpensive for those waiting to be allowed into the United States.

One of the most valuable features of Senda de Vida is the queue-management system. It keeps track of people waiting. People register their cell phone numbers when they arrive. When it is their turn, they are notified. Pastor De Luna grabs his bullhorn each morning to announce the lucky cell phone numbers from the first-come-first-served list. People gather, hoping for their turn. "You need to see the person when they heard their number called. My God,"[35] he said, remembering the excited faces.

American attorneys accompany the individuals to the halfway point of the international bridge. There, they are handed off to CBP agents who continue the asylum process. The pastor often

Honduran migrant children do schoolwork at the Senda de Vida camp in Reynosa, Mexico. The facility holds more than twelve hundred residents on any given day.

receives calls from those who have successfully made it to their destination. He passes the information on to those still waiting, offering hope to the hopeless.

Pastor De Luna works to create a more humane and fair process south of the border. He works daily with CBP to create an orderly and respectful transfer of asylum seekers. "Call me, tell me how many you want, and let's walk there,"[36] he says, referring to the process of accompanying immigrants halfway across the McAllen-Hidalgo International Bridge. Pastor De Luna is grateful to individuals and organizations who donate funds to fulfill the mission of his enterprise.

Asylum Seekers Thwarted

As these stories illustrate, asylum seekers encounter a complicated web of obstructions at the border. The COVID-19 pandemic added yet another obstacle for those seeking asylum in the United States. In an effort to curb the spread of the virus, Title 42 gave CBP officers the authority to expel all migrants arriving at the southern border, including those seeking asylum. Since March 2020 more than 1.2 million people have been turned away. The order has been challenged in court as recently as January 2022. The Biden administration continues this measure as a means of controlling the pandemic.

CHAPTER FOUR

Decisions Made

Detained, released, or returned, asylum seekers face what happens next. Some must decide whether they can endure conditions south of the border while they await court hearings. Those released into the United States must rely on help from sponsors until they are able to find housing and employment. Being separated from their families back home causes additional trauma. Given the backlog of the immigration court system, asylum cases can last months, often years. During this time, migrants must try to navigate whatever paths remain open to them, and some have very few options.

Sent Home to Die

Some who seek asylum are denied and returned to their homes, only to face the very conditions they fled. That was the fate of Ronald Acevedo. He fled his home in San Salvador after members of the local gang threatened to kill him. His is a familiar story. On his asylum application, he wrote, "They already [killed] my friends, and they are going to do the same to me."[37] But there was more to his story, which complicated his claim.

As a middle school student, Ronald's friends pressured him into joining the gang. They told him if he did not cooperate with them, they would kill him or his family. So, he participated, occasionally acting as a lookout for gang members. He used his cell phone to communicate with them. But he never considered himself a gang member. He is unsure why they turned on him, but he became aware that they planned to kill him. That is when he left to seek asylum in the United States.

When asylum officers interviewed Ronald, he explained that his role had been minimal and that his life was at risk because he would not go further into gang life. But US Immigration and Customs Enforcement (ICE) labeled him a self-admitted MS-13 gang member anyway. They denied him bail and detained him in the Eloy Detention Center in Arizona for eight months while waiting for his case to be heard.

In court, Ronald's gang involvement, no matter how minor, became a barrier he could not overcome. Even when his lawyers produced a certified document from El Salvador's national police stating that Ronald had no criminal record, it made no difference. The judge ruled that the defendant could not be released because he posed a danger to his community. That is when Acevedo made a life-changing decision.

He called his father. "They're saying I could be detained for another six months, and that I have no chance of getting asylum. They're telling me it's better if I agree to go back to El Salvador,"[38] said Ronald. He felt he could never overcome his ties to the gang.

Members of the notorious MS-13 gang show off their trademark tattoos after being detained by police in El Salvador on August 10, 2017. Some migrants are fleeing gang violence in their country.

A few days later, officials presented him with a document. Ronald added his signature, officially withdrawing his asylum application. With that, he returned to his home and tried to remain hidden away. A few days later, he made plans to meet up with a friend. But he worried about his safety. "Mom, I'm afraid,"[39] he said.

Ronald never returned that night. His family did not report that he was missing because they feared that the gangs would be angered if they called the police. But after waiting five days, they went looking for him.

They found his body at the coroner's office. It was difficult for them to even recognize him. Ronald's family buried him in the public cemetery. Shortly after, amid further threats from the gang, the Acevedos found an attorney who helped them immigrate to Ecuador. His mother packed a picture of her son in her bag, wishing he could have started over again with them.

The Sacrifice of Self-Separating

That desperate times call for desperate measures is a truism for many migrant parents at the border. After fleeing unspeakable tragedy at home and exposing their children to the dangerous journey north, they must decide how much more these youngsters can take. In the camps, they call it *la separación* ("the separation"). Knowing that their children will not be turned back at the border because they are unaccompanied, mothers and fathers make the excruciating decision to give their children up in order to give them an opportunity for a better future.

This is what happened to Delmer Lopez and his ten-year-old son, Jose Armando. The two had been returned to Mexico to await their asylum hearing. The father and son struggled to survive in the squalid migrant camp in Matamoros, Mexico. They arrived in late summer, when heat, mosquitos, and lack of water and food made it difficult to survive. For months they endured the unsanitary conditions, but as winter approached, with temperatures dipping into the forties, Delmer made a decision.

No longer willing to subject his son to life at the border, he packed the phone number of José's mother, a favorite stuffed turtle, a jacket, and a passport into a small backpack and strapped it on his son. Delmer hoped José would reunite with his mother, who lived in Houston. Although the parents were divorced, it was the best place for the boy.

Delmer gave José a hug and a promise that he would see him soon. "I gave José five pesos to cross," he told a reporter. "He walked away and then turned around and waved. The last thing I saw was my son being escorted away by two American officials."[40]

Many parents have made the same gut-wrenching decision. "We do it because we don't want our children to suffer," explained Delmer. "This was the hardest thing I've ever done in my life."[41] For Delmer, it seemed like the right decision. Although immigration officials denied his asylum claim and ordered him deported back to Honduras, he still hoped to find a way to one day be with his son.

Seeking Sanctuary

People seeking asylum often must live with uncertainty about their future. For Hilda Ramirez and her eight-year-old son, Ivan, the wait for an answer lasted more than seven years. Their journey from Guatemala began in 2014. Hilda feared for their lives due to domestic violence and political unrest. So, she took what little money she had and paid a *coyote* to guide them to the United States. After a harrowing trek, they made it to the US border.

Border Patrol officers apprehended and processed them when they arrived. She failed the initial credible fear interview, but was given the chance to appeal in immigration court. In the meantime, authorities sent the mother and son to the Karnes Detention Center in Karnes City, Texas, for nearly a year because they could not pay the $10,000 bond. Eventually they fitted Hilda

FIFO vs. LIFO

Under many different US administrations, asylum policy followed a system known as FIFO—first in, first out. Once migrants had passed the credible fear interview, they waited in line behind others who arrived before them. Then they would proceed to immigration court for a final decision. The Trump administration changed that procedure. It instituted LIFO—last in, first out. By focusing on migrants who had just crossed the border, it expedited the decision-making process. This enabled the government to quickly return recently arrived migrants without risk of losing them in a complicated system that takes years to unravel. It addressed the front of the line, but it meant that those already waiting for years added even more time to their delay in pleading their case in court. The backlog continues to grow, adding more uncertainty to an already difficult process.

with an ankle bracelet to monitor her whereabouts and released the two to a local shelter. But with ICE agents sweeping the country, rounding up asylum seekers who had lost their cases or faced possible deportation, Pastor Jim Rigby of St. Andrew's Presbyterian Church opened his church's doors and offered sanctuary to the Ramirez family.

Sanctuary offers protection for those sheltering inside churches, hospitals, and schools. These are considered sensitive locations. Government agencies, such as ICE, usually do not enter or make arrests inside these facilities. Individuals are protected as long as they remain inside.

The Austin, Texas, congregation outfitted a Sunday school classroom to serve as a dormitory for their new tenants. People donated clothing and signed up to bring meals to the pair.

The church was definitely a better place to be than the detention center; however, the Ramirez family had little freedom. Twenty-four hours a day, Hilda remained sheltered within the church building. Because of his age, Ivan could attend a nearby school, but he could do very little else. Hilda could not risk leaving the premises.

Hilda would not give up her fight. Her lawyer repeatedly filed stays of deportation—a legal move to keep them from being sent back to Guatemala. The courts denied every request. Hilda and Ivan lived the sanctuary life in fear, but with hope it would one day end.

Only after President Biden's inauguration did good news arrive. In the spring of 2021, they received a temporary stay of removal. Although only good for one year, the Ramirezes are hopeful that with the support of advocates, they will be able to receive permanent resident status. For now, Hilda is attempting to get a work permit, and Ivan has qualified for a special immigrant juvenile visa. "I'm very happy that I'm at least able to go outside as I have always dreamed of," Hilda told reporters. "And I'm happy that I can go and see my son play soccer and take him

> "I have fought many years to keep us together, and I will keep fighting to make sure our family is not separated."[42]
>
> —Hilda Ramirez, asylum seeker

to the park, but I know that the fight for us continues. I have fought many years to keep us together, and I will keep fighting to make sure our family is not separated."[42]

Succeeding and Serving Others

Often, the end of the story for those seeking asylum is unknown. Many who have shared their experiences with reporters during the process prefer to fade into the background and not call attention to themselves. It is difficult to find many success stories. But one asylum seeker, Soledad Castillo, has shared what she learned from the process to help others.

No longer feeling safe in Honduras after suffering physical and sexual abuse at home, fourteen-year-old Soledad appealed to her father who was visiting from Hayward, California. She convinced him to take her along when he returned to the United States. The month-long journey was filled with long days of walking, riding crowded buses, crossing a desert, and going days without food or water. Along the way she witnessed and experienced robberies and violence, all the while hiding from immigration officials. She persisted and eventually made it to the border.

But Soledad's dream of what America would be like quickly changed. Her hope of returning to school, which she had left at the age of eleven, would have to wait. Her father demanded that she go to work at a nearby laundry in order to pay him back thousands of dollars for the trip. She worked long shifts, from 7:00 a.m. to 11:00 p.m. Most of her paycheck went directly to her father, leaving little for herself or to send home to family. When her father suddenly decided to return to Honduras with his girlfriend, Soledad found herself abandoned, and authorities moved her into the foster care system.

She struggled for four years while living with foster families, but she managed to return to school and eventually received her high school diploma. But the clock was ticking for Soledad. As a minor, living with her sponsors, her protection would end when she turned eighteen. Luckily, her social worker helped to get Soledad's immigration papers in order before her birthday. With her asylum case approved, Soledad was on her own. She had lawful permanent residency status in the United States, a Social Security card, and the drive to be successful.

After completing her degree at City College of San Francisco, she continued her studies and earned a master's degree in social work from the University of California, Berkeley. Using her life experience, Soledad now works on behalf of others seeking asylum and has become a voice for youth in foster care. Soledad writes, "I'm not telling my story to make people feel bad or pity me. I want us to work together to make changes in the system."[43]

In an interview about what asylum seekers need, Soledad said, "Start seeing us as human."[44] She asked that others see the individuals and listen to their stories and not make assumptions. "I am not a bad person. I came here to survive, to do better in this world, to help my family and other people."[45] Soledad Castillo is an example of one person's success in the asylum-seeking process. But her journey from Honduras to lawful permanent US residency is only one chapter in this young woman's story.

Ways to Improve the Asylum Process

The immigration court system is heavily backlogged with 1.3 million asylum cases. It takes an average of four and a half years for a hearing date in court. For asylum seekers, that means years of living in limbo—stuck between the persecution endured in one's own country and the long wait for a decision that leads to more permanent safety and refuge in another. Many say the system is broken. But there are practical ways to improve the process.

One suggestion is to allow asylum officers in the Department of Homeland Security to handle asylum cases instead of immigration courts. According to Doris Meissner of the Migration Policy Institute, "The majority of Central Americans who arrive at the border are not going to be eligible for asylum, but some percentage will be."[46] To identify those cases with merit, asylum officers could be authorized to make decisions based on the credible fear interview. No referral to the immigration courts would be necessary for those who pass. However, those who fail the interview and face deportation could still work through the courts. An updated system to quickly process those who truly are in need of refuge could make a big difference.

Another way to improve the system is to focus on the sixty-five thousand asylum seekers remaining in Mexico under the MPP. The Biden administration continues to fight against this policy,

A US Border Patrol agent uses a video bank to spot migrants trying to cross the border illegally near Yuma, Arizona.

"Out of Sight, Out of Mind"

Title 42, the public health order that denies admission to the United States due to COVID-19, enables CBP to turn migrants away at the border without any investigation. MPP, commonly referred to as "Remain in Mexico," returns asylum seekers across the southern border while they wait for their hearings. Both of these policies keep migrants out of the United States. "Seeking asylum in the United States is a legal pathway. And if people are pushed out, we won't see them—out of sight, out of mind," explains Yael Schacher of Refugees International. Videos and pictures of squalid tent camps paint a desperate situation, but these conditions are not happening on the US side of the border. Both Title 42 and MPP pass the buck to the Mexican side of the border to deal with those awaiting asylum. These policies benefit the US government by keeping asylum seekers out of public view and perhaps off the minds of US citizens.

Quoted in Sarah McCammon, "'Remain in Mexico,' the Trump Era Policy That Haunts the Biden Administration," *All Things Considered,* National Public Radio, October 22, 2021. www.npr.org.

claiming it defies US and international obligations to provide a safe place for asylum seekers to wait. Changes to the MPP now allow people with health issues, the elderly, and others with vulnerabilities, including those who identify as LGBTQ, to be admitted to the United States. More is being done to provide legal assistance, better security, and safe transportation for those forced to wait in Mexico. Additional immigration judges to hear those cases are being added. But more must be done.

Finally, the United States must focus on the root causes for seeking asylum. The individual stories reported in this book are each unique. Some of the conditions, such as domestic abuse, lie beyond the control of the US government, but others can be addressed. The US Department of Justice is cracking down on the trafficking of illegal drugs. Its Anticorruption Task Force focuses on drug cartels, gangs, and human rights violations in Central America. Creating policies that alleviate the impact of climate change on this region can also address a root cause of why people seek asylum.

People will continue to come to the southern border. Whether they are forced out of their homes by gang violence, economic hardships, domestic abuse, political strife, or climate change, those in desperate need will look to the United States for help. They have endured violence, hardship, exhaustion, and hunger. Many who crossed seeking asylum have become productive members of society, working in the most essential jobs and adding to the diversity of America. They see the promise that life in the United States holds.

SOURCE NOTES

Introduction

1. Quoted in Marissa Peñaloza, "Haiti Faces Disasters and Chaos. Its People Are Most Likely to Be Denied U.S. Asylum," National Public Radio, October 16, 2021. www.npr.org.
2. Quoted in Peñaloza, "Haiti Faces Disasters and Chaos."

Chapter One: The Root Causes for Seeking Asylum

3. Quoted in American Immigration Council, "Asylum in the United States," June 11, 2020. www.americanimmigrationcouncil.org.
4. Quoted in Kate Morrissey, "Protecting the Most Vulnerable: What It Takes to Make a Case Under the US Asylum System," *San Diego Union-Tribune*, February 24, 2020. www.sandiegounion tribune.com.
5. Quoted in Morrissey, "Protecting the Most Vulnerable."
6. Quoted in Steven Mayers and Jonathan Freedman, *Solito, Solita: Crossing Borders with Youth Refugees from Central America*. Chicago: Haymarket, 2019, p. 142.
7. Quoted in Mayers and Freedman, *Solito, Solita,* p. 146.
8. Quoted in Mayers and Freedman, *Solito, Solita,* p. 146.
9. Quoted in Mayers and Freedman, *Solito, Solita,* p. 146.
10. Quoted in Mayers and Freedman, *Solito, Solita,* p. 147.
11. Quoted in Mayers and Freedman, *Solito, Solita,* p. 147.
12. Quoted in Mayers and Freedman, *Solito, Solita,* p. 147.
13. Quoted in Lidia Terrazas, "One Cuban Migrant Family's Long, Perilous Journey to Freedom," Cronkite News, July 14, 2020. https://cronkitenews.azpbs.org.
14. Quoted in Terrazas, "One Cuban Migrant Family's Long, Perilous Journey to Freedom."
15. Quoted in United Nations High Commissioner for Refugees, "Human Lives, Human Rights." www.unhcr.org.
16. Quoted in Katie Benner and Caitlin Dickerson, "Sessions Says Domestic and Gang Violence Are Not Grounds for Asylum," *New York Times,* June 11, 2018. www.nytimes.com.

Chapter Two: The Journeys

17. Quoted in Morrissey, "Protecting The Most Vulnerable."
18. Quoted in Morrissey, "Protecting The Most Vulnerable."

19. Quoted in Refugee and Immigrant Center for Education and Legal Services, "MPP Is Still Happening and There's a New Threat," October 19, 2020. www.raicestexas.org.
20. Quoted in Mayers and Freedman, *Solito, Solita,* p. 136.
21. Quoted in Terrazas, "One Cuban Migrant Family's Long, Perilous Journey to Freedom."
22. Quoted in Terrazas, "One Cuban Migrant Family's Long, Perilous Journey to Freedom."
23. Quoted in Mayers and Freedman, *Solito, Solita,* p. 148.

Chapter Three: At the Border

24. Quoted in International Rescue Committee, "Crossing the Border: A Young Central American Mother's Story," June 27, 2019. www.rescue.org.
25. Quoted in International Rescue Committee, "Crossing the Border."
26. Quoted in Colleen O'Dea, "Separated at the Border, the Story of Andrea and Her Son José," NJ Spotlight, December 22, 2019. www.njspotlightnews.org.
27. Quoted in O'Dea, "Separated at the Border, the Story of Andrea and Her Son José."
28. Quoted in O'Dea, "Separated at the Border, the Story of Andrea and Her Son José."
29. Quoted in O'Dea, "Separated at the Border, the Story of Andrea and Her Son José."
30. Quoted in Hilary Andersson and Anne Laurent, "Children Tell of Neglect, Filth and Fear in US Asylum Camps," BBC News, May 24, 2021. www.bbc.com.
31. Quoted in Andersson and Laurent, "Children Tell of Neglect, Filth and Fear in US Asylum Camps."
32. Quoted in Veronica Stracqualursi et al., "What Is the Flores Settlement That the Trump Administration Has Moved to End?," CNN, August 23, 2019. www.cnn.com.
33. Quoted in Mallory Falk, "The Asylum Trap: 'They Returned Us to a Country We Don't Know," KERA News, October 19, 2020. www.keranews.org.
34. Quoted in Refugee and Immigrant Center for Education and Legal Services, "MPP Is Still Happening and There's a New Threat."
35. Quoted in Todd Bensman, "Inside a Most Unusual Mexican Migrant Camp," Center for Immigration Studies, November 22, 2021. www.cis.org.
36. Quoted in Bensman, "Inside a Most Unusual Mexican Migrant Camp."

Chapter Four: Decisions Made

37. Quoted in Kevin Sieff, "When Death Awaits Deported Asylum Seekers," *Washington Post,* December 26, 2018. www.washingtonpost.com

38. Quoted in Sieff, "When Death Awaits Deported Asylum Seekers."

39. Quoted in Sieff, "When Death Awaits Deported Asylum Seekers."

40. Quoted in John Burnett, "'I Want to Be Sure My Son Is Safe': Asylum Seekers Send Children Across the Border Alone," *All Things Considered*, National Public Radio, November 27, 2019. www.npr.org.

41. Quoted in Burnett, "'I Want to Be Sure My Son Is Safe.'"

42. Quoted in Mary Tuma, "After Years Sheltered from ICE by Local Churches, Immigrants Get Reprieve," *Austin (TX) Chronicle*, April 23, 2021. www.austinchronicle.org.

43. Quoted in Mayers and Freedman, *Solito, Solita,* p. 36.

44. Quoted in Laura Wenus, "US Policy Frustrates Honduran Immigrant Who Crossed the Border at 14," *San Francisco Public Press*, June 28, 2021. www.sfpublicpress.org.

45. Quoted in Mayers and Freedman, *Solito, Solita,* p. 37.

46. Quoted in Franco Ordoñez, "Biden Administration Considers Overhaul of Asylum System at Southern Border," *All Things Considered*, National Public Radio, April 1, 2021. www.npr.org.

ORGANIZATIONS AND WEBSITES

Amnesty International
www.amnesty.org
Amnesty International is an international nonprofit nongovernmental organization focused on human rights. It is committed to holding governments responsible for their treatment of asylum seekers, refugees, and other displaced people.

International Rescue Committee (IRC)
www.rescue.org
The IRC helps people affected by humanitarian crises to survive, recover, and rebuild their lives. The IRC assists asylum seekers on both sides of the US southern border, offering meals, clothing, transitional shelter, and travel coordination to recently released detainees.

Project Amplify
www.project-amplify.org
Project Amplify is a nonprofit created to provide legal protections for child migrants in government care. It works to share children's stories about their experiences in detention and amplifies those voices through the arts. In addition, it works with policy makers to ensure that the human rights of these children are upheld.

Refugee and Immigrant Center for Education and Legal Services (RAICES)
www.raicestexas.org
RAICES provides free and low-cost legal representation to underserved immigrant children, families, and refugees. It provides bond money for the release of detainees, help preparing for credible fear interviews, and assistance with resettlement and navigating the asylum process.

Southern Border Community Coalition (SBCC)
www.southernborder.org
The SBCC is a group of more than sixty organizations along the US southern border whose purpose is to ensure that border policies are fair and humane, to improve the quality of life in the affected communities, and to support rational and humane immigration reform. Its website offers data and a variety of graphics related to the asylum process at the border.

Books

Rachel Ida Buff and Alejandra Oliva, *A Is for Asylum Seeker*. New York: Fordham University Press, 2020.

Judy Dodge Cummings, *Border Control and the Wall*. San Diego: ReferencePoint, 2020.

Steven Mayers and and Jonathan Freedman, *Solito, Solita: Crossing Borders with Youth Refugees from Central America*. Chicago: Haymarket, 2019.

Jacob Soboroff, *Separated: Inside an American Tragedy*. New York: Custom House, 2021.

Juan Pablo Villalobos and Rosalind Harvey, *The Other Side: Stories of Central American Teen Refugees Who Dream of Crossing the Border*. New York: Farrar, Straus & Giroux, 2019.

Internet Sources

"A Guide to Title 42 Expulsions at the Border," American Immigration Council, October 15, 2021. www.americanimmigrationcouncil.org.

Arelis R. Hernández, "Marooned in Matamoros," *Washington Post*, July 22, 2021. www.washingtonpost.com.

Michael Posner, "What America Owes Haitian Asylum Seekers," *New York Times*, October 4, 2021. www.nytimes.com.

Project Amplify, "Child Migrants Speak Truth to Power." www.project-amplify.org.

Maya Rhodan, "Number of Asylum Seekers Has Risen by 2,000% in 10 Years. Who Should Get to Stay?" *Time,* November 14, 2018. www.time.com.

Patricia Smith, "Will Ginger Get to Stay?" *New York Times Upfront,* January 7, 2019. www.upfront.scholastic.com.

United Nations High Commissioner for Refugees, "Children on the Run." www.unhcr.org.

INDEX

PICTURE CREDITS

ABOUT THE AUTHOR

Patricia Sutton is a nonfiction author and former middle school teacher. Her award-winning debut book, *Capsized! The Forgotten Story of the SS Eastland Disaster,* was published in 2018. She has a master's of fine arts in writing for children and young adults from Hamline University and lives in Madison, Wisconsin.